The Ghost Beside Me

Written by

Lee Hall

Text copyright October 2019

Published by

Lee Hall

All Rights Reserved by

Lee Hall

© 2019, Lee Hall, except as provided by the Copyright Act January 2015 no part of this publication may be reproduced, stored in a retrieval system or transmitted in any form or by any means without the prior written permission of the Author and Publisher.

This novel is a work of fiction. Names and characters are the product of the author's imagination and any resemblance to actual persons, living or dead is entirely coincidental.

Book Cover by Design For Writers

About Lee Hall

Lee Hall is an independently published author and playwright from the UK. He has a passion for reading and blogging while also supporting fellow authors.

https://leehallwriter.com/

https://twitter.com/lhallwriter

Books

The Teleporter

(The Order of the Following Series)

Open Evening

Darke Blood

Cemetery House

Plays

Hotel Doom – a one act comedy

Beauty & the Beast - a pantomime

Snow White and the Seven Dwarfs – a pantomime

Dedication:

This book is dedicated to the wonderful memory of Raymond John Berryman.

Known as 'Monty' or 'Mond' to many, but to me, he will always be Grandad.

Table of Contents:

About Lee Hall iii
Dedication: iv
The Ghost Beside Me:...vi
Introductory Note: 1
Initial Acquaintance: 3
Secondary Acquaintance: 18
So Forth Acquaintances: 29
Empty Spaces: 36
Finished Business: 44

The Ghost Beside Me

Introductory note.

The paranormal is a subject I hold with the utmost contempt and dismissal. Quite simply; I do not believe in such forces or phenomena and to entertain the thoughts of such is insulting to even the lowest form of intelligence.

My profession is numbers and figures; specifically accounting; something which is indeed fact and fact only where there is no room for deviations that rely simply on one's belief. There is no believing when it comes to numbers, they are either there or not.

I came to embrace this rationale for the duration of my formative years and into adult life. If I were to approach my profession with the same subjective nature as those do with the paranormal then I would be thrown to the cobbles and perhaps considerations would be made to lock one's irrational self away.

On the other hand it would be pointless to delve further into this account if my philosophy in life toward the paranormal remained as rigid as the formerly mentioned. Recently I have come to believe there are certain possibilities that exist where one's nature can be changed. We as people or vessels voyaging in this world can be shaped by the events in which we experience. Those who arrive in our lives even for a short time and those who eventually depart can certainly make their mark. I never imagined in a hundred years my own life would be affected by a being of the 'departed' persuasion.

Strange noises, unexplained presences, nondescript events, visions and midnight visitations are all something I thought to be wrapped up in the pageantry of fiction. Some even find comfort and consider such to be an appropriate companion with the season of joy and giving. We all know of those accounts or stories and I am the last soul to ever imagine that one would cross my path, Edward Neville; proprietor of fact, a soon to be senior accounts clerk and loner for most of the time, by choice.

This is my account in diary form of the events leading up to and of my brush with the paranormal. I assure you that everything in this account is indeed truth, I have aforementioned that I only deal in fact and that is all you shall find.

To achieve the true authenticity of my experience it is recommended that this account be read in a gradual manner by candlelight in the dead of winter.

- E. Neville

1. Initial Acquaintance

October 22nd

My passion for numbers and appreciation for the finer details of numeracy is a stark contrast to my detest towards most social orientated situations. This is fostered by the rather inadequate social skills I possess. The socially conscious mind must recede to attain such focus to the very fine bottom lines and discrepancies that I find daily in the profession of accounting. This is my present-day excuse and I shall admit that I am happy to be of the introverted persuasion.

If the evening commute by way of the 17:56 from London Paddington was depicted by way of a landscape painting, my presence would be in the furthest background. This is a place I am most comfortable, however, British travel culture in general isn't a sociable scene, something even I am able to sense. Dialogue from all corners is reduced to the uttering of a few words for the duration of a journey. This arrangement suits me well and therefore like clockwork I survive unscathed by the harm of having to talk 'small' during one's journey.

I have taken a room at 'Martha's House' located in the 'Greater' region of London which is just four stops on the Express. This quaint Tudor style boarding house is the residence of mostly other professionals such as myself. The elderly lady who owns the property boasts to include an evening meal every night for residents; something I shall consider partaking in even if this is a generous offer, I am stubborn towards social interactions.

All of my worldly possessions I transferred to the house over the previous weekend and so the short walk from the station was light although the October breeze contained a bitter bite. Leaves of fiery red and brown crawled through the street with the season's change in full motion whilst I glanced up to the three-storey house and my home for the time being. A warm orange glow of interior lamplight flickered through high windows and invited me towards what I hoped would be respite from the bitterness.

The warmth didn't disappoint after I turned my very own front door key that all newcomers receive. Upon entry to 'Martha's House' the sounds of mealtime chatter carried out from the dining room doorway; the rhythm of voices remained uninterrupted signalling I had made entrance undetected even after pushing the front door to. I stood on the tiled floor of the hallway and eyed the nearby stairs. Hastily I moved there and in the opposite direction of those voices. Of course every other step I climbed creaked like an old ship navigating itself through a storm but I had graced the first floor without being discovered.

Pursuing the first floor landing I followed the passageway as it double backed past the bannister and then along a trio of doors leading around a corner to a pair of steps. After an abundance of yet more creaking I had made my way through the quirky 'Martha's House' and to my door. Using another key, I let myself in to room '4'.

Everything remained like I had left it while a brief damp musk hit my sense of smell. My trunk sat idle at the end of a moderately sized bed straddled by a plain writing desk and chair on the right. With the light casting in from my still open door I located a half-used candle and brought my room into flickering light. After a sigh of satisfaction for successfully receding to privacy I made for the door and pushed it to a close. My eyes faced a shiny brass hook attached to the rear of the door and I eased off my overcoat with every plan to hang it upon this implement. Upon hanging my overcoat this hook appeared to wobble slightly and only moments later did it give way with the garment becoming a crumpled heap on the wooden floorboards.

Partially flustered, I scooped up my overcoat and faced a narrow door to the left; presumably a closet that had previously slipped from my attention. I gripped the brass handle that belonged to this entrance and a cold sensation hit me as it opened outwards while candlelight flickered into this hollow space. Efforts to find a suitable hanging device for my overcoat were to no avail within and so I turned and slung it over the foot of my bed. I then immediately pushed the closet door to a close and followed the bed's length where it's simple framework head sat snuggly before the window ledge.

In the darkened autumnal street below leaves began an abrupt migration with the whistling wind being their carriage. After a presumably hefty gust and shudder all around the closet door behind me gently opened. Yet again my gaze focused on the shadowy space and I made for it. Upon a brief inspection I closed it and then scooped up the fallen brass hook which had failed to support my overcoat. Before I could place it on or let alone reach the writing desk this unruly closet door yet again gently opened.

'Enough now,' I muttered and made my way to it.

With more force I pushed it shut and almost instantly it forced itself open with that musky coldness hitting me. Following a brief inspection, the handle mechanism appeared defective, although my credentials in the matters of ironmongery are hardly adept, that is my chosen diagnosis. To abstain the coldness which seemed to creep from this space and with no chance of the closet staying shut I took my discarded overcoat and hung it over the top of this permanently open door. It shall do for now.

October 23rd

My first night spent within the quirky walls of 'Martha's House' was indeed an unsettled one. Perhaps the transition from my former rooms to the current played some part; we are creatures of habit after all and this is without mention of the defective coat hook and closet door debacle.

Not long after I sat to finally scribe such events I found myself on the very brink of slumber. Uncharacteristically I set off from consciousness without supper. Perhaps the rumbling of an empty gut was indeed the reason for an unruly night's sleep. It appeared that every hour I would awaken just before my unconscious state of sleep reached any level of depth for rest.

A vivid memory plagues my mind; one of awakening with a gasp in the rather small hours. I recall the light being limited to deep shadows and being startled to see a tall figure stood at the extreme end of my compact room. Even in a state of dishevelment my eyes eventually adjusted to realise this figure was in fact my own overcoat resting upon the top of that unruly closet door.

By the time morning light cast through my drape free window I felt far from ready to face another working day. With my grog apparent, I lifted my weary self from an unsettled first night; a soon to be senior accounts clerk can sleep post-promotion.

Instead of my usual early evening routine of a solitary walk through Hyde Park I decided to take tea instead by way of the 'Royal', a grand but mostly sparse place where much time has been spent in creating a palace like ornamental hotel attached to the frontage of Paddington station. Even though I boast to have social inadequacies, there are some I choose to spend time in the company of, even if I am more of a passenger.

'You are looking weary as usual dear Ed,' the jolly Humphrey Hardwick said in between bites of a well buttered teatime scone.

'Tell me, are you 'too busy' to eat yet again? That firm will be the death of you old chap,' he added and slurped tea from his porcelain cup.

Before I could mount any level of witty defence Humphrey's words beat me to it, he was a man who possessed a daily quota of dialogue which needed to be said.

'You need only ask and I shall put in a word at the bank. They are always on the lookout for number minded souls.'

'Dear Humphrey, I feel as if my journey to senior accounts clerk is too far along for a change at present. It is simply too good...'

'An opportunity to pass up?' Humphrey retorted, he then continued with this bullish interruption, 'those are words you have been muttering since we were both apprenticed at that god-awful firm...' He suddenly eyed a passer-by before leaning forward.

'Excuse me Miss! May we have some more strawberry jam?'

The brute of a man I considered to be my closest friend pointed a sausage like finger towards a rather young serving girl who had stepped into his territory. She immediately nodded and scurried away.

'They never provide enough jam. You know in the west country they stress over the detail of a scone and such orders involving jam or cream. I have no time for such detail,' Humphrey snorted and took another loud slurp of tea.

This time my wit was armed and ready, 'and that my friend is why you are in banking and not accounting. Detail is indeed key," I said with a brief smile.

'Very true,' he chuckled.

'But Ed there are other pursuits in this life. You need a lady to marry, then your worry will be eating too much and not enough. Is there no one you have met?'

'I believe there is more to women than marriage and getting fed Humphrey. They are complex and sophisticated creatures who I prefer to watch from afar,' I admitted knowing my excuses.

'Of course, and I would be lost without my Mary but there is no company like the companionship of a significant other. You would make a fairly adequate husband Ed.'

Perhaps dear Humphrey meant well, but saying well is a totally different matter although we shared a momentary chuckle. For a brief time, I forgot about the apparent pressure I bear upon myself in most social situations, I found solitude in forgetting and I suppose as a species we shall do anything for a quiet life.

The train journey out of London was indeed uneventful yet again. Partly due to choice and partly due to my own inner thoughts. Good old Humphrey was right, companionship is what I need but I feel as if my situation can compare to candle without a source of ignition. Perhaps I just need a social spark somehow.

Upon reaching the door of room '4' 'Martha's House' I discovered a folded pair of drapes sat by the threshold waiting for me. Presumably a small gift from the elderly lady who owned the house and although they appeared to be partially battered, they shall suffice.

My final task of the day faced me by way of recording today's events and again an urgency to retire overcame me with hopes of an adequate slumber. 'Adequate', that word again!

On this occasion I made sure to drape my overcoat on the chair as opposed to the closet door.

October 24th

Again I awoke in the small hours full of grog and with only partial consciousness. Something must have disturbed me and upon being awakened I abstained from opening my eyes initially; there came a feeling and expectation that I wasn't alone in room '4'. I eventually opened my eyes but alas nothing. Just the shadows of my compact chamber stood unaccompanied. Although this sensation seemed strange, sleep hastily overcame such reservations.

The day consisted of no notable events, from a dull morning commute to avoiding any eye contact at all costs.

Eventually I found myself facing the door of number '4' 'Martha's House' and on this eve, I was greeted with a tray of supper awaiting my return. The cheese and bread accompanied by wine I found to be a surprise well received. There are forces in this house which I gather have grasped my perhaps anti-social approach; an approach I choose simply because I have found no success in such situations.

With a more so encumbered gut than usual, that being one full of cheese and bread washed down by wine, I decided to retire for the evening.

October 25ᵗʰ

Even though I had found a deep slumber it abruptly and momentarily ceased at what I presume to be a similar time to the previous night. While feeling inconvenienced more than anything my bravery to open both eyes arrived promptly. Only shadows faced my tardy gaze and my mind began a wander toward an explanation before sleep found me.

Every free moment on this day I spent relaying that exact moment of awakening, my urge to find rationale and reason unending. Just what is routinely disturbing my slumber? Did my encumbered gut have a part to play on this occasion? Is this a disturbance of my own doing? Is this due to change in my usual habitual situation? Could it be as simple as a late arrival to one of the neighbouring rooms? A stray creek in the already famously noisy anatomy of 'Martha's House'? Perhaps both in succession for the same number of nights? Coincidence could play into such a possibility.

Even after that second 'event' I found good rest, perhaps this fair amount of sleep is fuelling one's mind to an overactive measure. If only my focus could point towards a more productive matter.

Casting back to dear Humphrey and his words on companionship remain in the very bowels of my own mind, tucked away beside irrational fear is a desire to address the fact I am stubbornly set in the ways of alone. In an attempt to find distraction from the 'situation' in room '4' I set myself the ever so daunting task of exchanging all but a few words to a fellow express passenger during the evening commute from Paddington.

Just the thought of such created a heightened sense of anxiety. My chest tightened and courage inside somewhere began to pluck itself up. I stepped onto the express with high hopes to just exchange a greeting with a solitary passenger only to find the carriage deserted. Instantly I found relief in retreating to alone and my thoughts of what could possibly be behind these night disturbances.

Tonight I am ready to discover more and as I finish scribing today's events my thoughts have wavered towards a very realistic explanation. 'Martha's House' is indeed an older dwelling, I am hypothesising that there is something more than just creaky floorboards or closing doors to blame. I may not be alone after all, my theory points towards a mouse! Seeing as my mind is awake, I intend to keep the rest of my person awake until an answer presents itself.

Post journal entry update – I have unknowingly omitted a minor detail about the décor of room '4'. There is compact fireplace that sits beside my bed adjacent to the writing desk. Tonight I have lit a reasonable coal fire to provide more light than usual, it is with hope that this source of illumination keeps me from slumber.

Post journal entry update two - The fire's warmth pulled me into a deep sleep although I awoke at what appeared to be a time that surpassed the usual hour of disturbance. Early morning light bleeds in through battered curtains. Better luck tonight perhaps.

October 30th

Time tends to have a way of moving with such haste and can appear to go unnoticed. A number of days have passed since my last entry and like clockwork the disturbances have persisted at a time I have pin pointed to be around the hour mark after I retire. This is only a rough estimation as it is difficult to fully gauge even when going by the rule of pocket watch.

Visions during sleep appear to be vivid and full of memories from people and places of yesteryear. It brings a small level of comfort while I attempt to make this compact chamber my own. Every so often I see another vision, one of that empty express carriage and with it comes a feeling of anxiety to simply strike up a single word even without audience. My urge to not be alone grows for some unknown reason I am yet to fathom. This is truly a battle and the battlefield consists of my choice to not socialise against being alone.

Alone is becoming a barren type of hell as of recent and I know the act of being social will lead to a reward or perhaps some level of happiness. If I could just break away from the shackles of that internal torment I have created that imprisons my confidence. Just the idea and thought of tackling this enigma of feelings spirals my own self into a deep sadness, hence my lack of entries in the past days. With journal entries comes a reflection of matters that weigh heavily upon me.

In an attempt to abstain from such ill feelings, I know there is much to be positive about. My health and occupation are in fine form. A soon to be senior accounts clerk has much to find the light in. Edward Neville has an abundance to boast about but our fixation in life and what we don't have can create unnecessary problems which in turn lead to an unfulfilled existence.

A known default for avoiding such problems is to discover a distraction and on this eve I became enthralled in such a thing. The other tenants of 'Martha's House' I overheard during one of their many rambunctious supper gatherings by way of the dining hall. Specifically, their conversational subject matter pointed towards myself and my reclusive nature, hence why I decided to loiter upon entry to the house.

'Perhaps the poor fella is yet to meet her,' said the voice of an older gentleman.

'Number '4' has seen too many tenants for it to be a coincidence,' he affirmed.

'Or he just isn't acquainted with the ways of ale, much like the others,' another gent said with laughter erupting.

'Most drunks fail to navigate this house in their state, but I am not a believer in this *'Silver Lady'* of yours. There is no truth to the matter if you ask a person of rational taste,' a well-to-do sounding lady admitted and at that moment a deathly silence followed.

Perhaps they could sense my prying presence, so I covertly converted my loiter with haste up the stairs knowing which creaks to avoid.

My conclusion from their conversation, if you can class it as that, is one of mystery and partial apprehension. They appeared to be exchanging nothing other than a level of gossip best suited for the schoolyard. The mention of a *'Silver Lady'* only stirs my rational and plain imagination. I deal in numbers which are fact, not hear-say.

October 31st

I can only describe my latest sleeping endeavour as Shakespearean! To elaborate, my deep state of unconscious found itself accompanied by visions of my own self in room '4' of 'Martha's House'. This peculiar occurrence seemed to be a vision within a vision very much like the bard's habitual resort of presenting a play within a play.

Before fully retreating to those depths of slumber I felt a state of euphoric comfort which seemingly brought a smile to my face, I knew just then sleep faced me imminently and the space I drifted in was where I sensed something else. It felt as if I was accompanied by another. Eyes felt like they were watching me and a feeling like nothing I had ever known paired with it. In that moment I had never felt so certain that I was no longer alone in the room.

An overwhelming sense of this force watching me gave me only feelings of comfort; this culminated at the very summit of this sleep fuelled drift and then a furiously deep slumber abruptly followed.

On this night my belief points towards what has been disturbing me and it may have partially revealed itself or one's self at the very least. This is indeed no mouse or a late arrival to the house. There is no sound of creaking floors or the wind outside. My theory points towards it having a presence of its own; a unique type of aura.

Even though I am not sure what I could see or feel on this night there is something else in this chamber and with it I had made an initial acquaintance.

2. Secondary Acquaintance

November 5th

We are upon the month of ultimate lethargy. Those once powerful autumnal colours have faded to grey on the wet cold streets. It's cold and dark or both. Umbrellas and overcoats fill the spaces before me while my mind appears to always be within deep thought. Although I admit to being well rested my appearance is of a man who is tired and dishevelled. Faces glance to me with concern as opposed to the transparency I once found solitude in.

On this morn particularly I found myself on the receiving end of a piteous offer to sit on the bustling express carriage full to the brim of rain sodden commuters. It is apparent my appearance is raising some concern.

The working day merged into a series of still frame portraits of myself monotonously going about my duties because back at room '4' of 'Martha's House' contains a curiosity that has commandeered my undivided attention.

I spend my time craving for sleep and it's depths just so it can be disturbed. My hopes point towards discovering the owner of those eyes which I felt upon me in that state of drifting. Tonight like the previous nights they could be revealed.

This is no longer a matter of fact and numbers which is gospel to all of my core belief. There is something I have found to exist on a grander scale in this plain we call life. Feeling or emotion, I'm not quite certain but this 'disturber' has me ready to believe, so much so, other matters I find to be daunting no longer bare that effect.

My departure to the station this eve was made with haste, I didn't even stop to think about the social repercussions of assisting an older fellow with an abundance of impossibly heavy luggage onto the express. Of all the busy professionals around on the cold wet platform none of them seemed to notice another soul clearly in need. The guard's whistle seemed imminent and still this fellow struggled with an expeditions-worth of possessions. The social implications I usually ponder were non-existent while I lent a helpful hand to this man. I had carried out this act of kindness and unknowingly defied my usual traits.

'Bless you kind sir,' the older gent said, his tone grateful and jovial. He followed my lead onto the carriage while I carried the majority of his luggage.

'You are indeed welcome,' I replied not even feeling as if I had endured an ordeal. I nodded to him and scurried to find a vacant seat in the bustling rush hour carriage.

I took rest by way of a seat next to one young lady who appeared to be immersed by a book. My mind momentarily browsed the thought of daring to strike up a conversation or even make a polite comment until a crashing realisation brought my memory back and I remembered who I was, careful now, I thought. At that moment her gaze met mine and in somewhat of a panic I turned away blushing. Perhaps another time, after all I have other matters to attend this evening.

Upon recording my express 'heroics' I faced my place of slumber with an eagerness to be disturbed.

November 6th

It seems that eagerness has hampered all real chances of finding suitable sleep. The later the hour became, the less tired I seemed to grow. My body tossed and rolled like the unruly tide of stormy high seas. Sleep was minimal and I found myself fully awake by the early morning.

What followed was a day I mostly spent in my own mind shrouded by the haze of sleep deprivation and a frustration for not being disturbed.

A station, the cold, a train. The blurry residence at the accountancy firm, a station, the cold and a train.

I took my usual tray of supper left at the foot of my own door and dozily ate. My hope is to find sleep on this eve, disturbed or not I am in debt to rest and it must be paid.

November 7*th*

Sleep came swiftly and earlier than usual. The debtor of rest was looking to collect and that it did. The small pile of coal inside room '4's' mantle warmly glowed as I turned towards the dark.

Suddenly I awoke in the small hours. The coal I now faced reduced to nothing but a few embers and my focus entirely on the feeling of a presence before me. I was too tired on this night for any kind of interest and fully turned away.

'Not tonight, Silver Lady,' I muttered dreamily without any real sense of control or choice. A dreamless slumber ensued.

This moment I have only just recalled after a day that consisted of no notable events. The bed behind me beckons and as I finish this entry it is indeed an inviting notion.

November 8th

Yet again a deep sleep consumed me until I was awoken by a sharp scratching sensation at my feet. Gasping in surprise I rose to see nothing at my feet or underneath the blanket which only partially covered me.

That warm glow of coal beside my bed provided enough light to pull me towards a full but dishevelled consciousness. Was there something in my bed or was I just imagining such things? Initially I fumbled in a panic but the more awake I felt the less I believed it to be anything more than my own toenail scratching my other foot. Consciousness fosters reality and when I am awake fully the vines of imagination and what could be fall away into the background.

Is this 'disturber' just an essence of my own thoughts manifesting itself by the vessel of loneliness? Does my mind take strives further to fashion it into a work of fiction? Does solitary confinement garner such behaviour? These apparent 'disturbances' only occur upon reaching a certain level of depth within my slumber. Am I only able to reach and communicate in this state because it's my own mind? That sensation of drifting or floating which I now refer to as being 'under' is an existence just before deep slumber can indeed be a euphoric experience and also quite fearsome.

Is this all just trickery of my own mind? I desire to know just that.

Hearing what the other tenants spoke of around the dining table some time previous may have just fabricated by selective hearing of my own desires.

My chosen affliction to be alone could be manifesting a being from a subconscious imagination. Am I just spiralling into madness? Even if this so called 'disturber' exists on some level I know for a fact when I dreamily called to it in the fashion of a dismissal there came no response and what good is having an acquaintance with something that doesn't exist?

November 9th

My belief of this manifestation's existence has been derived from within my own imaginings I am certain. Last night came no feeling of disturbance and still I awoke as my slumber approached the 'under' state. Is this because my inner conscious has adopted the routine of expectation? Will this be a normal circumstance from now on?

The hypothesis I am swaying towards consists of a man with an empty lonely heart creating an illusion of such to simply fill a void. Only conscious reality could possibly fill such a void, this much I know. My focus must return to career based thoughts and aspirations of a soon to be senior accounts clerk.

November 13th

Those thoughts of fantasy wash away further every night without disturbance. I am building up belief that this so called 'Silver Lady' is just fabrication of the mind.

Even though I continue to awaken upon the summit of slumber I haven't felt the eyes of a disturber upon me for some nights now.

Time can be spent in better fashion and to be immersed in work is to forget.

November 15th

On this morn my restful slumber remained until first light in what I see as a small miracle. Upon the slow voyage of awakening, when the mind is sensitive, in the very bowels of thought there is the feeling of partial loss. The question I face is simple. Did my mind find regular stimulation when this 'disturber' preyed upon me?

These thoughts of ill nature dissipate when full consciousness arrives, I have other focuses.

Nearly a month has passed since my residency in 'Martha's House' began. Every day that passes of recent, room '4' feels emptier and emptier and without a certain life. Have I turned away the soul of this room in the form of a 'disturber'? There is an essence of my mind that feels some remorse for how I have shunned what could have been something other than what is just an empty spaced occupied sparsely by a writing desk, a bed and not much else.

Still I spend my day receding away from social situations of every persuasion. Those days of wishing to spark a simple conversation feel far behind. Have the effect of disturbances experienced in this room masked the anxiety I face when talking with others? Did I perform better with such things in my life? A feeling in my gut tells me I may have turned away something meaningful. My attention now turns to enticing this 'disturber' out of the silence.

Even if I have constant quarrel with my own belief, the now 'silent' conditions in room '4' appear to be more disturbing than the previous state. Above all, this 'disturber' filled a lonely void.

The apparent 'force' that once disturbed my slumber I feel has been turned away due to ill thoughts and belief of my own doing. These are words of a man who considers himself one of rational thought. E. Neville; a proprietor of numbers and fact has been caught in his own storm of inner belief. Even though I have a desire to think there is something more than silence in room '4', the common denominator is indeed myself yet again.

Even those not of this mortal coil cannot bare to entertain me. Who would want to? I am closed off from the social plain that exists around me. My true motives for such coldness is historic and a fact I do not wish to explore. Roots to some problems have no relevance. Situations are what they are, including this matter.

November 16th

Last night I bore my ill thoughts until slumber. At first an anger overcame my existence with frustration soon following. This formidable partnership eventually floated from the front of consciousness and I swayed towards that feeling of 'under'. It was at that moment of true vulnerability a resonating dull vibration emerged, an effect that truly baffles my search for any type of descriptive word to fully justify it's happening. This sound was and is like nothing I have ever heard before.

Were my eyes open or was this semi-slumber state just a vivid dream? The surroundings I faced with familiarity, the partially open closet at the end of my bed with the light low and almost blue. The coal fire beside me stood reduced and dwindling to ash. From where that partially open closet door stood and with my potentially asleep vision a figure stood.

Was this just my overcoat draped over the door? Instinctively my belief attempted to find rationale and I glanced to see my own overcoat draped over the nearby chair.

Still the indescribable vibration resonated all around and this figure gradually approached floating just above the floor, in my mind came no feelings of fear but a curiosity. In the dark almost blue light this mostly grey appearing outline journeyed closer. I could make out what I gather to be a thick grey or possibly silver material clung to a shrouded face. The figure's entirety stood draped in a veil of sorts and this figure, the figure of a woman floated towards me.

'I thought, I had turned such things away,' my voice said dreamily.

'You did,' the reply came, feminine and soft, gently hypnotic.

The dull vibration ceased when this ghostly woman revealed her face. I could only make out basic features. Her flesh pale and dark hair arranged in a braiding.

'Then how are you here?' I asked with a suspicious curiosity.

'Those ill thoughts you have of one's self...'

Instinct urged me to interrupt her prying words, she had been listening to my thoughts, my own private thoughts. This state of partial slumber didn't discriminate against my usual quiet self, I felt bravely curious.

'What of those ill thoughts? They are mine and mine only, what is your quarrel?" I asked.

'I have no quarrel,' her soft voice called to me.

'Then state your motives for persistently disturbing my sleep?' I ordered.

The irrational side of my persona had mounted a defensive mode I never realised existed. My words sounded malicious even if I had no real reason to feel attacked. The unknown can show a persona's true colours.

'I've hardly been persistent as of recent,' her voice said with just an essence of defence and then she continued, 'we shall grace the subject eventually although I do not wish to disturb you if that is what I have done.'

I could feel a sadness in her presence and tone which seemingly engulfed everything. This silver apparition began a hasty retreat.

'No, please,' I begged.

'Perhaps we have begun this second acquaintance badly," I added sitting up.

'Second acquaintance? We have just met, sir.' Her image momentarily stopped in retreat.

'Call me Edward, and I believe we have met previously and partially perhaps.'

'Partially?' the woman asked.

'I've felt something in this room before. As a man of rational thought, I assure you Miss. Being a man of numbers and a soon to be...'

'Senior accounts clerk. So you keep saying,' she said her tone now gracing humour.

'Well Edward, if this is our second acquaintance will you entertain a third?'

'Of course, Miss. And possibly a fourth, a fifth, a sixth and so forth.'

'Then tomorrow we shall begin our so forth acquaintances,' she said and turned away, just before she did my eyes focused to her light red lips that smiled. A feeling of happiness multiplied by one thousand thundered through me, so much so I almost forgot to respond to this late hour visitor.

'Very well Miss," I said.

'Call me Molly."

And 'Molly', the pale apparition, or the Silver Lady vanished into the blue shadows.

3. So Forth Acquaintances

November 17th

I eventually awoke in a disturbed and dishevelled state on this morn. My bed and person unkempt while light of the grey persuasion bled in through battered curtains.

Throughout the day my mind was occupied and all thoughts were seemingly infected by the matters that unfolded on the night previous. Although by now my persona has developed a system in showing a 'business as usual' front to whoever I encounter, I still cannot help but appear to be in a hypnotised state. Hypnotised by 'Molly' and driven by a desire to know more about this other occupant of room '4'. I appreciate this account may have taken some grand steps towards finer appeal and this is exactly how I feel towards the subject of night-time.

This day unfolded with my rational belief system attempting to steer towards the thoughts that this scenario could all be an elaborate dream. Logic would suggest that a mind spiralling into the madness of loneliness could 'invent' such imagery. Does 'Molly' exist?

Yet again I look forward to my hour of slumber with that question on the forefront of urgency.

November 18th

'Of course I exist,' a dreamy voice called to me while I lay in a state of 'under'; where some senses are heightened while and others are dulled.

'Must you play with my doubts?' I questioned. My distant feeling body made attempts to find an internal compass and gather it's conscious bearings.

'In a fashion yes, lay still Edward and allow this disturbance to be brief,' Molly said, her voice calmly commanding. Even in my distant state, I found an ease in her sound.

I followed her instruction by remaining deathly still. My body faced away from where I presumed she stood. Her presence I could feel even though she was an apparition.

'Am I permitted to question your existence Molly? Any logical soul would do the same. If I cannot lay my eyes or touch upon something, then is it really in this existence?' I asked.

'There are forces in your world and mine that exist but cannot be seen or touched,' her voice said to me.

It was at that moment my numb body felt a light almost miniscule depression on the surface of the bed.

'Even with this meeting of sorts, I still cannot grasp the logic of this situation or your visitation' I said even though my words were of a disparaging nature, I only meant them in the most curious of senses.

'Visitation as opposed to disturbance. There is belief in you after all.' I could almost hear the smile coming from her words.

'Without course to harm you with words might I ask what part you have in the somewhat fictional fashion you appear? Does my life and attitude towards such require change? What message do you bring to me Molly?'

A brief but deathly silence filled the room. Had I caused insult to the only force living or dead that had fully conversed with me for longer than a simple greeting?

'The message you search for I hope you find through our so forth acquaintances. Sleep Edward, I shall return to you yet again,' her voice said and trailed from me.

'Will there be a clear answer in any of this?' I asked and turned to see nothing but a shadowy writing desk. Shortly after and before any rational thoughts came to me, I found a deep slumber.

November 19th

All day I have spent in deep contemplation. The morale of this situation has changed state; from initial belief of said situation to questioning of a deeper nature. Why has Molly the 'Silver Lady' chosen to reach out to me? Does something of an internal nature require drastic change? Must I be influenced by her to improve my outlook upon this existence?

Like any situation which requires audit, I resorted to consultation from a soul with a permanent existence. The wording of how I would browse this subject would need to be precariously thought out. My counsel came in the usual form of Humphrey Hardwick and yet again our setting of the 'Royal', although on this occasion it appeared much busier than our previous encounter.

After a long tenure of listening to my dear friend present his quota of spoken words, a moment between subjects had finally arrived, so I chanced it.

'Tell me Humphrey, what do you know of the forces that stretch beyond the boundaries of our own mortality?'

He paused for no less than a moment.

'Not a lot. My Mary is the one who aligns herself with fiction in our household,' Humphrey admitted.

'But do you believe in the existence of such forces?' I probed. My tone and body language attempted to suggest I was simply and casually enquiring.

'It is a subject that hasn't graced my thoughts,' he said.

'A first for you perhaps?' I said with an attempt of wit that earned but a slight grin opposite.

'An encounter with forces beyond mortality is only something I have heard others relay back to me. Such events tend to be more believable depending on the availability of scotch and the likes. My question to you dear Ed is why?'

Internal thoughts had whisked me away until Humphrey's raised voice pulled my conscious back to the conversation in hand.

'Ed!'

'Yes Humphrey, that was my query to you, why?' I asked.

'Why what exactly?'

Before our joint confusion ensued, I snuffed it out.

'Never mind. I'm just rambling,' I said with more thoughts flooding my mind.

Even though our conversation on the subject was brief and no result transpired, a thought did strike me. Perhaps Molly is the one visiting me in search of change.

November 20th

'I do not wish to pry Molly, but may I question your motives for these visitations?' I asked in that familiar partial sleep induced state.

Her presence I could feel beside me as her answer emerged.

'I could ask you the same Edward. Have you not thought about proceedings from my side?' Molly asked, her voice growing more and more human with every word.

Indeed, her point was valid. My tenure in room '4' may have been shorter than hers, but it still didn't answer the question of why she had emerged from the shadows.

'You carry a valid sense of logic. Something I have an appreciation for,' I said with my eyes finding hers while she sat at the end of my bed. A smile began to form from her pale features.

'Is logic what you seek from every acquaintance?' she softly asked.

'I haven't many acquaintances. Discounting you makes it lesser so,' I admitted.

She looked away with a smile that flowed into a soft giggle. A reaction I cannot recollect anyone having for any words ever spoken by myself.

'What is it you find humour in Molly?'

'You claim to lack socially even though your persona has a natural style which finds a way to compliment me. Whether you know it or not Edward, that is what I find intriguing about you. I am drawn to it, I am drawn to you,' she said, and I could feel her reaching out to me in a figurative sense.

'Style' is never a word I would associate my social skills with and normally my subconscious would default to triggering social or anti-social barriers in this situation, but around Molly, it appeared to be nowhere in sight. In the company of this acquaintance I held a desire to converse and an urgency to express words in a humorous fashion. This is a feeling I found to be uncanny, an almost curiosity pushed me onwards. I had to know more.

'Is intrigue your sole motivation? I was unsure forces of your persuasion carried such curiosities,' I said and without giving Molly a chance to answer, more words flowed from my mouth.

'Is there an ulterior sub-conscious motive that keeps you here Molly?' I asked. My confidence grew with every word.

'That is a question...'

I sat up and interrupted her hesitant words with more theories of my own.

'Did something happen in this very room. A curious somewhat bare room, until the likes of your presence filled it. Is the reason behind your presence of the sinister persuasion? These are normal grounds for a case such as this. Were you a victim?'

'Stop Edward,' she defensively commanded.

A wave of instant guilt overcame me. I had ignored all social barriers with this newfound confidence and in doing so I must of hit a 'paranormal nerve'. I had overstepped a boundary.

'I must apologise for probing,' I grovelled.

'Logic and my search for such always gets the better of my curiosity.'

I felt a desperation to see her eyes meet mine, but they never did. Her head bowed and turned from me.

'What if neither of us need to find logic in this matter,' she said.

In the moment I looked away in search of a response, Molly's image had dissipated and like clockwork a wave of exhaustion pulled me into slumber.

4. Empty Spaces

November 24th

Some days have passed and my memory continually recalls every failed acquaintance of the life I have led. I am but a fool being haunted yet again by my own thoughts. The brief presence of Molly is now just a regretful recollection that has replaced her. She's gone. Yet again, like every situation I have been the root cause to its failure. My desire and urge pushed everything too far. A desire to no longer be alone has led to just that. We were only a matter of days into our fragile acquaintance.

Even though I carry a lingering feeling that Molly's existence carries some deeper reasoning, I am starting to believe it carries no relevance. Even a ghost I have somehow managed to push away. My mind is at a complete loss. The past days entries don't exist because like room '4' they contain emptiness.

Molly may have been the promise of something positive in my life. Even if these encounters were brief, the distinct lack of further encounters with her heighten the true sense of loss.

What if this relationship, no matter how absurd, belongs in this existence? What if I were to put the logic of numbers and accounts aside? What if I were to simply embrace the opportunity for a true companion and take it at face value? Even if Molly's existence stretches the 'usual' boundaries, what are boundaries in such scenarios like this?

The Silver Lady of Martha's house may be my one and true opportunity for something more than an acquaintance. I am far beyond the reasoning of her existence now. Perhaps I should just believe.

November 25th

November's cold grip dominates the empty spaces caused by the absence of something I don't fully understand. Although our encounters were brief, my conscience thinks otherwise.

I have begun to accept Molly shall not be returning. If she was a creation or even a manifestation of my own imagination by way of loneliness I have still failed. How can one fail their own thoughts? A process once I considered absurd, much like this journey.

Through the murk and fogginess of this cold cold month is a faint glow which contains my aspirations to become a senior accounts clerk. It seems that glow which sits upon an unknown horizon moves further and further away. I must trudge harder towards such aspirations and find a way to resume 'normal' service.

There is promising word that the firm will be addressing staff on the matter of promotional aspirations by the end of this week. Even in these times of distraction, I must be, I have to be a frontrunner.

November 30th

All aspirations of becoming a senior accounts clerk have fallen through my own loose fingers. I have simply been a fool. My time will not be wasted in dignifying the names of those who have conspired against my efforts. Introversion shouldn't have any relevance in the subject or the ability I possess in the profession of accounting.

Being told to 'smile every so often' is the lowest form patronisation I have ever felt. News of this failure broke in a public and distasteful manner. Anger washed over me instantly and I must have expressed this obviously as my eyes met the regretful soul who picked me to the post. Of course, E. Neville carries a certain standard of manners in every situation and so I happily extended a hand in congratulations while a deep sadness consumed my very existence.

Everything I find belief in seems to have slipped away.

Rain forms into a downpour.

I lay in a bed of solitude with thoughts and thoughts only. A burning regret washes over me for allowing my own mind to spiral towards thoughts that distracted my true aspirations. I was foolish for letting this happen, truly foolish.

December 1st

The night of my darkest day felt seemingly cold and empty. As the month of grey reached its pinnacle, I faced a search for slumber with difficulty. It took some time to reach that state I've described as 'under'. Now this was a state overpowered by a deep feeling of sad emptiness until a brief and noticeable vibration emerged. This could only point to one outcome; a needed arrival.

An inconvenient depression in my bed threatened to pull me from this half slumber.

'I am here Edward,' her hypnotic voice said. The voice I have longed to hear. That internal woe began to fade with the sound of her.

My eyes opened to meet a face with pale and somewhat sharp features. Her cheeks defined and lips ready to speak again. An image I had never witnessed this close. She truly was a beautiful sight.

My stare wandered to her elegant neck and a ghostly glowing demeanour that felt entirely open.

'Indeed you are,' I said with a genuine happiness.

'I must thank you for returning Molly. And for giving this acquaintance another chance. There is so much I wish to say and tell...'

Her soothing words calmly interrupted my perhaps erratic reach for an apology.

'I know. We shall reach that destination soon. Now I am ready for you to ask of my motives,' she said.

Having been burned by my own urges before and learning from the experience, I knew now how to handle such delicacies. And so my words formed.

'I have learned motives in this world and yours do not matter. The fact you are beside me is all that matters,' I said garnering an instant reaction from Molly by way of a surprised and ghostly gasp.

Even with my body in the state of 'under' I forced a hand towards the image of hers.

'If only I could lay here with your hand in mine, I would,' I said with an overwhelming sense of sleep taking over my body.

Just before that moment of slumber I was certain I could feel the light and cold weight of a hand resting in mine.

December 2nd

There is only a portion of my own reasoning that finds recent times to be absurd. I can imagine anyone looking in from the outside to be aligned with such thoughts.

Even now when my emotional 'inner self' finds a great need for 'Molly' I am immersed in an almighty battle and struggle to believe she even exists in a sense. Are these events anything more than fabrication and manifestation caused by my own loneliness? She only seems to appear when gloom is at a level of maximum and when I am in a state described as 'under'.

This lack of belief is contrasted to another feeling, one I cannot fathom. It seems to erupt within my own gut when I think of her. This is not a physical type of pain but more of an impending want to be beside her. We have only been acquainted on a limited basis so what is this feeling, this foreign sensation?

Through all of these usual conflicts of belief nothing will satisfy me more than to simply 'feel' Molly's presence.

The day after my darkest I survived and exhaustion of the emotional persuasion led me to early retirement.

December 3rd

My slumber endured the complete duration of the night and into early morning. The very first emotion I felt upon awakening was shrouded in a sadness for not being 'disturbed' if that's what I class it as now. Perhaps like before she read my inner thoughts and chose to abstain her presence on this occasion in order to allow respite. Molly has shown compassion previously and so that is a theory I shall certainly entertain.

A slow and cumbersome day then unfolded with misery being the main theme. My mind was very much hopeful that she will appear on this night. I long for her. And in my hours of want I spend addressing the fact I felt her hand in mine for all but a moment the last time we were acquainted.

December 4th

Long and you shall receive because just before my conscious slipped 'under' I felt startled by the arrival of an extra weight landing beside mine.

'I have been expecting you' I said dreamily, and happily.

'Your longing for me I can feel Edward' she said, her voice a pleasant orchestral rendition to me.

'What is this we have Molly? Something beyond acquaintance and further than the boundaries of friendship,' I remarked to receive a soft chuckle in reply.

'You are never without question of circumstance,' she said through a smile.

Once again, she had found comedic value in my words, an unintentional wonder on my behalf.

'You are indeed a curious soul Mr Neville.'

'It is my nature to pursue fact, but I also know our arrangement stands beyond the reaches of logic Molly.'

'Arrangement? Why so formal sir?' She asked again finding a laughter; a sound hypnotic to my own heart.

'I shall try to reduce my formalities if you do promise to visit me every eve,' I proposed.

'Dear Edward, your nature requires no reduction, it is what drew me to you. I shall visit you every eve if you so wish.'

'I do so wish. The thought of such fills me with a happiness like no other. I have required the unique counsel of someone like yourself for some time' I said with an attempt to softly say I needed her.

'Someone like myself? You speak as if I exist as a mortal like you.'

'You do. To me you are real Molly, whether you doubt that carries no relevance. Living or other, I have never been in the company of someone quite like yourself,' I said.

My words were presented with a level of honesty I have never shown to anyone.

'Perhaps being a mortal is an existence not for me. What if I were to join you in your, condition?' I asked knowing the absurdity of the question.

'Then you wouldn't be the Edward Neville I have come to know. I am quite fond of this 'arrangement' and how it exists in its current form. What if I had no desire for it to change? What if we both needed each other as we are? In these circumstances we have found a balanced relationship,' she said.

'I certainly know that I need you Molly,' I admitted in a tone best described as heavily induced.

My final memory of that eve consisted of a particular cold feeling which seemed to take hold of my open hand. I used all my remaining partially conscious strength to grip the force and the hand of a soul I was getting closer to.

5. Finished Business

December 10th

Molly has kept to her word and promise. Every late eve since her pledge I have had the wonderful pleasure of her company. My inability to keep up with this journal is due to the truly wonderful distraction her soul has provided me with.

Our conversations have ranged in a plethora of subject matter. We are two souls afloat in twilight, our unison of being there for one another. The wound of not being a senior accounts clerk seems to have been healed and is indeed a lifetime away.

Every night feels like another fresh insight into this now blossoming relationship of mostly conversation. Even though winter's cold grip rules over most surroundings, internally I am enduring the summer months, it keeps me warm while I make my way in and out of London every day. For possibly the first time since youth I am looking toward the season of joy and giving without contempt.

My feet walked upon cobbles as I took in the seasonal surroundings of a nearby market that straddled the entrance to Paddington station. Amongst the hustle and bustle of rushing professionals I still managed to take in the sights and smells of mulled beverages and cooked meats. Something I now know as cinnamon overpowered the airwaves briefly. Those who passed me carried smiles and laughter; something even I craved to join and I know back at room '4' there is someone waiting for me whom I can exchange such with.

Frequently Molly and I hold hands; a concept seemingly impossible but I assure you as the sky is grey; this is fact. Every meaningful relationship finds a working formula and we have found ours.

These foreign feelings inside my own gut are commonplace and point towards a word I am still finding an understanding for; love, or at least affection. My desire to see Molly has moved towards an urge to now share with her how I truly feel. I wish to tell Molly that I have come to love everything about her. All questioning of such matters previous have disappeared into the background and I must share my feelings.

A once proprietor of lonely is now the keeper of a soul full to the brim with a wonderous affection for the spirit of Molly. In that background where such questions hide is contrasted by a foreground which is now full of answers. Just how has E. Neville come to love another in this life? The answer; by stretching my belief beyond the formalities that are described as 'normal' which I now haven't a place for. I've chosen to look beyond this mortal world and past certain 'logic', the reward simply put, is her.

On this eve I have decided that I will tell Molly how I feel and perhaps if we can successfully hold hands then is there no reason why I might possibly be able to steal a kiss. How times have changed. A journey of ill beliefs, solitude and discovery; all of which is culminating in the concept of kissing a ghost.

I must tell her how I feel.

December 11th

As per usual the Silver Lady in question came to me in the late hour. Her image glided toward me in that dark almost blue low light. Her usual position she took to lay beside me and before I could even attempt to speak, she began.

'Please Edward, I can feel what you have been longing to say, but I must urge you not to,' she said with a fearful quiver.

'What is the matter dear Molly?'

'I wish for this, for us, to never change, I wish for nothing to move forward but for us to remain how we are.'

I could feel the pleading in her tone.

'You know everything must move forward eventually Molly. The days, the months, the seasons. Our relationship has always been in a state of forward motion. Have I been too overbearing with my affection for you?' I asked, my words precariously chosen, I could not see her turn away like before.

'A soul like you could never be overbearing Edward. The quarrel lies with me. Although we have never needed to acknowledge why I am here, there is a reasoning, a reasoning that I fear shall find resolve if we move further,' she said and still I could sense in her fear and concern in those seemingly broken words.

My dreamy 'under' state did not help the situation of urgency, in fact it hindered or ignored its presence. Damn my urges.

'But Molly, I will proudly admit that I am a man who loves...'

'Please Edward!' Molly shrieked.

'There are forces beyond recognition and understanding that govern this situation and I don't want to lose you. I have only just found you,' she added.

'There is something you aren't telling me Molly and although that doesn't really matter, what really matters is that I am present. I have no forthcoming desire to depart from Martha's house anytime soon,' I said and offered my hand.

'I trust your word always but I do not trust the forces beyond. My fear is that I will be taken from you if our relationship is to continue along the current path.'

Not only did I hear conflict in her voice, but I could also feel woe. I had to find a way to resolution.

'Very well Molly. For your sake I will not push in any direction. If you desire to remain in this same wonderful space, then I welcome it because this is truly a wonderful space.'

My eyes began to close, a force I could not resist. A cold weighty sensation pushed upon me. Molly had gotten closer than ever. Sleep then ensued.

December 12th

All attempts to process my last conversation with Molly fell flat numerous times on this day. Luckily, this failure to process had a viable reason. My distraction came in the form of dear Humphrey whom I had met at our usual place, 'The Royal'.

'You appear to be more with-it Edward, do tell me her name good sir?' He asked with those rosy red cheeks pushed up by a jovial smile.

My gut urged me to make a partial admission.

'Molly,' I said.

'But I am afraid there are some complications in the matter,' I hastily added.

My companion snorted before replying,

'There always is upon the initial stages but, hazarr to you sir. I am relieved for you Edward. Anyone who wishes to spread rumours of particular subjects will seemingly fall flat in their efforts from now on. Ha!'

'Indeed,' I said in defeat.

'When will I have the pleasure of meeting this Molly?' the curious gent said opposite me.

'Not for a while. We are in the preliminary stages of what I hope to be something that lasts. For now you shall have to rely upon my vivid descriptions,' I admitted to receive what could only be described as an approving chuckle.

'Of course old fellow. Such pleasures must only be shared with the use of language. As a fellow of numbers like myself this may require some extra efforts. Now I must extend an invitation to you Edward. The season of joy is near and you must join myself and Mary on the day. She has convinced me to play host this year to her somewhat unbearable rabble of an extended family. My immediate bargaining piece for this displeasure is the request of your presence to not only accompany me with moral support but to act as a social buffer,' Humphrey explained. There was an offer of invitation extended within those words somewhere.

'Social buffer? Compliments are indeed in the eye of the beholder Humphrey but of course I would love to join you,' I said.

Just some mere weeks previous this would be a decision weighted by the anxiety of placing myself in precarious social situations. My answer emerged without thought. This is just another observation that proves having Molly in my life is but a precious thing.

My return to 'Martha's House' was later than usual but still Molly came to me.

'A social buffer? And you say this man is your friend?' She asked, her tone carrying curiosity, a contrast to the previous night.

'We have a specific friendship. We did apprentice together. Does this arrangement bother you?' I asked.

'Not at all. It is a social setting in which you belong Edward. I am proud you have already accepted his invitation,' Molly said fondly.

'And I am in debt to you or shall I pass blame to you for developing my character for the better?'

'I wish to apologise for last night's antics Edward. I have no desire to root or confine you in anyway. It is absurd for me to wish we would stay in one place forever. For now, dear Edward, sleep. Soon I hope to share with you my story...'

December 13th

On this day Molly's words haunted me for the duration. With the limited experience in the field of paranormal studies that I have, one can only imagine her tale to be harrowing. If this is what she is prepared to share with me then I am prepared to reciprocate and share with her how I truly feel.

The cold of day eventually cast itself away into an even colder night. 'Martha's House' shuddered in its entirety while the firm winter's wind blew outside my window. Every now and then it would almost whisper its way through some deep crevasse or opening in this aged dwelling in which I resided. The door to my chamber rattled in the gentlest of nature, causing only alarm on the first occasion.

On this night came the culmination of my tenure in room number '4'. A ultimately final feeling came over me even before Molly made her appearance in the shadowy dark blue space in which we shared a residence. But without failure the Silver Lady appeared, her image and shimmering dress more apparent, perhaps from the weather situation or my eyes had finally trained themselves to see her better.

'Edward, it is time,' her dreamy voice called to me.

'I am ready Molly, you can trust me with anything,' I said fighting away this 'under' state which gripped my being.

'Please join me,' I requested, and she obliged although on this night she remained in the upright seated position instead of choosing to lay beside me. Her cold hand found mine and the lightest of weight I could feel in my palm. Even with our contrast in states she carried an apprehension or almost nervousness which I could somehow feel.

'There is much that I cannot recollect or even have an appreciation for. Time is something my existence is impartial to. I am not of the mortality you possess Edward. My feelings towards this existence I have is one of negativity and confinement,' she admitted, my agreement in the form of a sleep fuelled groan.

'Of course,' I said doing my best to fight unconsciousness.

'This routine we have found has given me great pleasure Edward.' Her perfect face and stare found mine.

'You have broken my routine previous and broken it for the better. I am afraid that this situation is a temporary one,' her words of truth flowed into a silence. Was this a dismissal of sorts?

'My story is one of tragedy. When you questioned my motive and logic, I revisited my final days as a mortal in a solitary painful swoop. Afterall I am a ghost, a word you have refrained from use, in politeness or perhaps denial but in that word contains the truth,' she said.

I continued to watch her in the dark blue shadows of our setting. In all the time I stared she resembled a soul who was in great pain and discomfort. At that precise moment even with my disadvantaged state of sleep I came to realise Molly's story didn't matter. I just wanted that look of pain to leave her.

'I needn't know the finer details Molly. The why's and the how's, they solve nothing and carry no relevance to our unique bond. You have shown me that, and so much more,' I admitted while sitting up with urgency.

'You must know Edward, or we will both forever be left in a state of the unknown. This is a void in which I reside with a premise I embrace as a spectre who haunts this room with malice. That was until I approached you,' she said.

'What makes me any different?'

'Everything,' she breathed before continuing.

'For all but a while our souls have been aligned. My story is one of deep loneliness, much like yours. I saw myself in you. I knew then that I had to attempt to reach you. And you received me like nobody ever has.'

'Anyone would be intrigued for the promise of having something more than solitary confinement and deep loneliness,' I said bolstering the case that I am nothing special in this world.

'You never let go of your belief for me,' she said and began what I gather was a pouring of her heart's feelings by a way of words.

'Once I thought I had found love. I was to be...'

'You needn't tell me Molly, please' I interrupted. It is not that I couldn't listen to her sadness shrouded words, but I didn't need to. My hand tried to grip hers harder.

'You needn't relive old memories,' my voice blurted in an attempt to justify my initial interruption.

'All of this. What we have. It thrives on the basis of now and now only. Our pasts and perhaps even our futures carry no relevancy Molly. Please for the love of god don't think that I do not care for your story, of course you occupy this room for a reason but...'

'Does it really matter why?' She asked rhetorically and in defeat because she already knew the answer.

Our eyes met. A look of pure realisation faced me, it was not a malicious look but more a of a curious stare of wonder.

'You must know that I haunt this room because it is where I chose to leave my mortal existence behind. That is all I shall share with you about my history, but you must also know this existence in which I currently reside; if you can call it such, was one of loneliness, sadness and true woefulness. That was until I found Edward Neville...'

A subtle smile appeared across her near perfect face, my internals lurched in admiration and again Molly's words formed towards more compliments to me.

'You are an exceptional soul Edward. You chose not to socialise for reasons I cannot fathom. Social situations are where you belong. Giving others pleasure with your dry wit and rigid reasoning. You are a character that is wasted by just conversing with me,' she admitted and lowered her head. I could no longer see that smile as more words were about to flow from her, they were intertwined with a gradual sadness.

'Perhaps there are forces beyond all recognition that pushed me to take the path I did. I feel now that it may have always been the plan. There is another feeling inside me that you may not understand, she said with a quivering voice now upon the verge of tears.

'I love you Molly. I truly do,' I said.

All decision making pointed towards me saying those words and as they were announced her face of apparent horror looked to me.

'Those damned words. You are too good for me Edward...' Her image momentarily faded before brightening more than ever. A dull vibrating began to resonate all around the bed.

'Our acquaintance and it's journey has damned me I am afraid. Edward, I am fading...' She held out both hands in front, their imagery even though bright was indeed fading.

'I don't want you to go Molly.' I tried to lurch forward with urgency while fighting my incoming state of slumber.

'It seems I may not have a choice,' she said with even her voice seeming distant.

I didn't want her to go and something inside my own gut told me her departure would be permanent. Even though it pained me to accept that fact, I carried a desire to look past the agony of separation and say some words of truth and meaning because although it may have been brief our time together meant everything.

'You've lived your life Molly, before and after mortality. You have also given me mine,' I said with that vibrating completely filling the room. I reached out and she struggled to move closer to me. Forces beyond our recognition were taking her.

'I love you too Edward, always. This arrangement has been strange but very real...'

The brightest of glows filled room '4' accompanied by that vibrating which in turn became a stiff breeze. A coldness engulfed everything, a paranormal feeling putting all of my senses on edge. These were forces pulling us apart. Molly looked to this glowing with pure dread. More words came to me in an instant.

'You are too good to spend your existence in just one room Molly,' I called to her.

'As are you, remember that Edward,' her voice said softly but it cut through every other reverberating sound.

'Your business is finished here but I must ask for one final request?' I asked. She fought the brightness and with what appeared to be great effort Molly the Silver Lady faced me.

'Yes Edward, anything.'

'I would much like a kiss from the ghost beside me.'

Her glowing aura rushed to me even though the powerful force that had filled the room seemed to pull her. This force I could feel grew in every step she took to defy it.

She fought on and came to me. For just a moment in time I felt the softest, coldest press on my lips. Then came the dark and then came the silence...

***

Even love stories of the simplest nature can appear to be absurd from the casual observer. My tenure at 'Martha's House' ended shortly after Molly had 'moved on'. Only for a brief time were we aligned by our solitude and loneliness.

Even in the deepest darkest of voids one can find something truly worth having in life, or death. Upon reflection, my acquaintance with Molly was spent truly in the moment and that is the ultimate wonder of love; a force that doesn't discriminate, a powerful force that defines us all. Perhaps nothing before or after matters, just the moment existing itself is enough.

As I sit writing this epilogue of sorts my desk is strewn with accounts to be approved by the senior accounts clerk of the newly formed Hardwick and Neville accountancy; that senior accounts clerk being yours truly.

Time is of the essence as it's not all work that I have planned, I am to meet this evening with a wonderful young lady who could be described as an acquaintance of the mortal persuasion. This is the E.Neville far removed from the old with a belief that forces can stretch between this life, death and everything in between. I am a better person for it.

I shall close with this; some forces are worth believing in. Even though my residence has changed I still find myself in that familiar 'under' state of slumber with a feeling someone is looking at me with nothing but adoration.

I can only reciprocate by believing that she is beside me, always.

Authors Note

This story is about a lot of things and ghost stories in particular have always captivated me; that is ever since my Grandfather told both me and my brother the story of his childhood encounter with the 'Grey Lady' of Cranford Park. He recalled this story while we sat in the peaceful church graveyard one afternoon in that park. I was probably 8 years old at the time and of course my parents probably weren't too pleased but I shall tell you now I was never scared once, just captivated by the concept of ghosts and the ghost my Grandfather saw was real. Even after all of these years have passed since he left us (13 to be precise, Grandad would find humour in that) his influence never left me, whether it's laughing at my own jokes; which I can proudly say I got from him or being very much aware of every Friday the 13th, and that is the true message of this story, people and the mark they make on us never truly leaves us.

Even though 'Molly' passed on, her acquaintance with 'Edward' shaped him for the better and whether or not she was real doesn't actually matter because he managed to overcome his social anxiety and loneliness. For a book that's an ideal situation solver but in reality there are people who suffer on a daily basis with anxiety, loneliness and depression.

These are subjects that we must talk about more if we are to overcome them. Whether it's in our daily dialogue or literature like this, everyone is stronger against depression and anxiety when they talk about it. In this day and age it's something we must strive to normalise.

Those who are familiar with my previous works will notice that this book is much shorter. My process for creating this story was a little different and in fact it involved just a pen, a notebook and an idea. I decided to come away from keyboards, screens and forever updating computers in an attempt to find my roots as a writer. This also meant I removed all expectations of a word count and focused more on the story which I am incredibly proud of and I hope you enjoyed the experience.

I would like to take this opportunity to thank my BETA readers for taking on this rather unique and strange experience. Without you I wouldn't have known that I had a story so thank you.

And to everyone else, thank you for reading my 5th book and please do leave a review.

If you are interested in reading more of my work you shall find a sample of my super hero comedy 'The Teleporter' following this note.

The Teleporter

(Exclusive Excerpt)

Written by

Lee Hall

Text copyright @ March 2018
Lee Hall
All Rights Reserved by
Lee Hall
Published by SatinPublishing

http://www.satinpublishing.co.uk

Recent Reviews of The Teleporter

'*You will laugh (a lot) and above all, find yourself rooting for the underdog!*'

'*A humorously crass story of a drunkard turned superhero...*'

'*A protagonist that works to earn your affections...*'

Chapter 1: First Orders

You know, I really love booze. There aren't many things in this world that I like quite as much as booze, and I'm not trying to tell the greatest love story ever told here. I'm just telling you now that I like booze. Whether that's beer, wine, hard liquor, cocktails, ale, shots, double shots, triple shots, drinks in hollowed out fruit, drinks in fruit-shaped glasses, pitchers, tankards, those big yard measure things, stout for the more culturally inclined and pretty much anything else I haven't mentioned. Oh, and probably moonshine if there ever comes a situation.

This isn't how I ever imagined starting my story, but I've dabbled in the world of writing stuff before, (I blog, occasionally) and I know how to be original. I imagine if we were ever to meet, it would be in low light, some smooth jazz would be playing, you know that type of music nobody owns but is always there in shitty movies? A bar wouldn't be far away, maybe there's already a drink in my hand, scratch that; there is a drink in my hand and I've already got you and myself a top shelf shot on order.

So, imagine this. The image of a cityscape fading into view over heroic music. Our main character is standing there atop of a sky scraper, and maybe a stern but gently dramatic breeze is blowing. It is taco Tuesday after all. Sirens rush by and our hero slings into action.

That routine won't fly here. Reason one, I can't fly. Plus, as far as I know, we have no big skyscrapers here in Bay Valley, so the cityscape thing goes out the window. Also, I'm not a good enough guy to go out and interfere with the Police not doing their job either.

A lot of these 'stories' lack actual motive, but you'll find a girthy supply of it here... mostly. You know these modern day 'super 'hero' tales (both dirty words), revolving around a distinct lack in the motive department.

Let's take the fine example of our local plutonium delivery person. I wanna say guy or girl, but let's be neutral here, you'll thank me later (preferably Nobel style). It's been a hectic weekday for our plutonium delivery person and the previous order didn't even tip. We've all got their flyers hanging around somewhere, so all of us know where we can get our radioactive goodness at a super low price. Enter a couple of low level thugs. They intercept our person and take away somebody's hard earned ionising goodness. Well, who's putting in the save? Because our delivery person clearly isn't trained in any way to handle stuff like that happening to him. The one-dimensional hero turns up and does some flippy or angry crap; there may even be a cool vehicle and it's all ultra-dramatic. Me? I get the bus, or cycle if I'm not too hungover.

Point is, that last paragraph to paraphrase, is my way of telling you this isn't your standard comic book hero story, it's just a book. There are no dead parents here. Mine live upstate, one's a Bank Manager and the other an elementary School Teacher. My pursuit of redemption comes from somewhere else, somewhere far more ordinary.

Nobody can relate to the brooding rich dude who decides to put on a cape, or that one red haired actress who wears a leather cat suit because we all know chafing is practical. What about the middle of the roaders? I'm not talking the average guy who becomes the unsung hero, but what about the guy or girl who never needed to be a hero? They've kept their head down and paid their dues. He might even live a life with no aspirations to have rock hard abs. He enjoys dessert, but will stand up for anyone of his friends who are wronged, not just about random dessert situations like a lack of sprinkles, but in general life situations.

What about the guy who leads a steady, risk free life in his mid-twenties? And by that I mean mid-twentyish. Okay, there may be a half-truth there, so we'll say mid to late twenties, look - just not thirty okay? I'm over it.

What if I'm neither a good guy or a bad guy? Maybe in life there aren't bad words, bad people or bad things; maybe there's just bad choices and intentions. And I'm not saying every asshole who is an asshole can be a saint. Some people never ever have good in them, but in concept they are hard to find.

Anyway, let's move away from our cityscape, we're down in the bar and our drinks are served. Pull up a chair and let me shoot the breeze for a while, because this is my story. The Teleporter. My real name is Kurt Wiseman and my shady memory takes me back to how this whole thing started; in a bar and probably where it will finish.

"You see Kurtis, you're still a young man and this is just your first rodeo. You've done what most people haven't, you've taken the first step."

I could always confide in Douglas Heaney; this older guy listens to all my woes and there's invariably room for that veteran father/mother figure in every story. A perfect role for that aging performer who maybe once wore the cape, but now deserves an Oscar. He always told me how it was and helped me to admit that I had a problem. And that's the first part of dealing with a problem, right?

"Now, for feck sake, drink your chaser," Douglas ordered. I watched him sink another whisky. He always turned more Irish when he drank, and he groaned whilst slamming down the glass.

I sat kind of slumped and let out a throaty belch. There I was, in 'The Drunk Poet's Society', a basement bar below my apartment building. A place where nobody knows your name, mainly because they don't show up. If there was a poetry scene it would be full of creative types and those pondering the written word, I know pretentious right? Now, there's just me sat opposite an older guy, originally from Boston, who used to write poetry.

"Okay, I got it." I slurred. Finally mustering up the courage, I gripped the tumbler and the ashy burning sensation hit my tongue.

"You're at the very beginning of this lad and the most important thing for you to do, right now, is move on," Douglas said. And he was right.

"I've been having some good ideas how." I half slurred. My fingers brushed towards a glass of stout.

"You see *'One Night'* was… was just my arrival man, it let the people know who I am." My head bobbed as I began to put the world to rights.

"*One Night in New York* was just perfect man. Not once did I ever track back, it was just me and a great graphic novel." I hiccupped as I finished tooting my own horn.

That's my graphic novel, in case you were asking. Two guys looking for revenge and who take on the mob in one rainy, gritty New York night. Their intentions; to collect the debts of the past. Sounds pretty cool, huh?

"Now with this next project, I'm gonna, I'm gonna…" I took a long sip of frothy stout.

"Sounds like you need more thinking juice. We should switch to beer, if we can get some fecking service in this place," Douglas barked from his slightly red face. He was up before I'd even finished my drink.

Across the empty bar he shuffled, past the many round wooden tables and stools; some of them with candles in big jars and others with those little electric lamps. Every available wall surface was taken up with either poetry verses in frames or books. I'm talking books in glass casings, books on shelves and quotes everywhere. Hell, even the enlarged front cover of my graphic novel stands on one pillar.

Guess I had better join him at the bar, it's probably my round and so I unhook my feet from the wooden legs and clumsily rise from my stool.

My evident drunkenness a few sips away from completely compromising my navigational skills. It's a nice distant hazy-type feeling, except for my upper right leg which seemed to be twitching. I should probably get that checked out.

"You see, this is why nobody comes to this place. Who would ever go to a poetry bar? You gotta have folks who like poetry to begin with," Douglas pondered loudly to himself. He waved a hand over to the small stage set up in the corner, a single spotlight shining over a microphone.

"It's only 'cause of drunks like me this place is still open." He slammed the bar.

"Well, I like it, even if it is several flights of stairs below my apartment." I said, pulling out my wallet and taking out some notes.

"Put your money away, it's no good when you're out with me." Douglas' red face glared my way. He then shuffled along the bar and headed behind it.

"Besides somebody has gotta drink the stock before it goes off," he grinned, grabbing two glasses from above.

"Come on Douglas, at least let me pay for my own drinks?" My hands steadied me as I gripped the bar.

"No Kurtis. If you had a plus one, then I would think about it. That lass you were with before knew how to drink." He chuckled in that jolly half Irish way and began to pour me another drink.

"I broke up with Jordan five months ago man, and yeah, the fact she could even drink you under the table was a problem. Not to mention the whole sleeping with another guy thing the entire time we went out. So yeah, I miss Jordy too." I said.

"You can be a smart ass sometimes, you know that?" he slid the beer my way.

"And where do I get that from?"

"How are the book sales going?" he asked.

"Well… they are not currently. I had the initial buzz and the whole 'hey, you wrote a book' thing and now? It's as busy as this bar," I grumbled, triggering a wheezing laugh from Douglas.

"I've put me life savings into this dump, but I can still laugh about it. Cheers," he said, and we clanged glasses.

"Tell me about the new book? What you gotta do is move forward, get more stuff out there."

I took a big swig of fizzy goodness and composed myself. Again, the leg twitching came but it didn't stop me talking to the 'one man press conference' that was Douglas; the only guy interested in my work.

"Well, you see Douglas, I've done the whole gritty New York mob revenge story. This time around, I'm thinking comic book hero. Maybe even a duo, but instead of good guys we've got two bad guys," I said.

"Comic book heroes with the whole bad guys angle, huh? Sounds desperate to me," Douglas said, "but you follow your heart and your thoughts. I did, and it got me to this place and there were some good in between times. Life is a tree, you start at the top…

'Here we go again with Douglas' analogy of life,' I thought to myself.

"You start life atop of this grand tree and hit your knackers on every branch on the way down to the ground," I said, finishing the man's famous outlooking quote on life. My Irish accent wasn't as authentic, no matter how much stout I'd had.

"Don't forget when you finally break onto the ground a dog comes and pisses all over you," Douglas said.

"So, remember, life is all shit anyways and you gotta make your best at it, son," he added inspirationally.

Well, inspirational to me anyway. And he was right, again.

It was then I decided to fully knock back the beer and go do something with my life.

"Monday means a new week, and today is Monday, so it's time for a new frickin' start," I stated with a sharp gassy belch. I stepped back and stood proud.

"Hear, hear!" Douglas said, with a delicate raise of his glass.

Just as I was about to blow out of that joint, another breeze blew in. Five or six high pitched loud voices cruised toward me and the bar.

"Another?" Douglas asked.

"Yeah, one for the road," I said and shakily grabbed a stool as the beer took effect. Curiosity held me back to see how this was gonna go down.

"Oh my god! They have like karaoke here!" One of them squealed, as they flocked towards the stage and microphone.

"It's for poetry," Douglas growled, with his no nonsense voice. I could sense the girls disappointment just as I caught sight of one of them wearing a pink sash.

Bachelorette party on a Monday night? I couldn't exactly discriminate as I gently sipped the new beer.

"But I can fire up the karaoke machine if you girls want?" Douglas called out and winked at me.

They screamed in approval as Douglas made his way to them. I faced the bar and left them to their own devices, but this was it. One drink and I'm heading back up to make another awesome graphic.

"Turk-wise! Is that you?" A high-pitched voice demanded.

I hadn't heard that name since High School and made all the more awkward as this bride-to-be was accosting me with it. Not that I had a problem with the attention, but looking at her I remembered the face and not the name. We are probably friends on that life-invading site and still I couldn't see her name next to a pair of apparent model style photos.

"Hey, you," I said half-heartedly.

"Now, I heard from somewhere that you have written a book?" The apparent model who used to go to High School with me asked.

"Yeah, it's a graphic novel, but yeah, not a big deal no." I said, only it's probably all I ever talk about.

"What about you, 'bride-to-be'? Apart from the obvious knot-tying activity, how's life been?" I added.

"Well I've been travelling and modelling…" Queue the snoring. Especially as her voice went up and down in a rolling pitch, please somebody, get me the damn mute button. Being semi-drunk allows you to skip scenes like this and so I did, she's not a principal character anyway, two scenes max. I successfully glazed over until she seemed to raise her voice to another decibel.

"Then I met this super awesome guy, so we're getting married!"

I've got an Instagram too, so does that make me a model? And that whole travelling thing, she probably went to France one summer and then got back with the asshole she went to Prom with. Why am I attacking this girl? Well folks, it's because what she said next was,

"I really want to read your book, you should totally send me one." This was followed by my usual glare of 'maybe you should pay for one yourself and help a guy out'.

It's not like I had put all my hard-earned savings into creating something I'd made from my own mind. I'm not bitter, I just don't like every conversation I have with someone I barely know turning into a pile of shit just because I'd made something creative. I'm not judging you, if *'One Night'* ain't your bag, I'm cool with that, let's get drunk instead.

"Come on, Stacy, we're gonna sing Rihanna!" One of her whining tag-along's said.

Bingo, that's her name; saved by a high pitch squeak.

"Well, congratulations Stacy," I said and took another sip of beer.

"Who's your friend?" The tag-along enquired as she appeared alongside Stacy.

"This is Turk-wise, that's what everyone called him back in High School. He used to make these goofy comics and sell them. Now he's published for real," Stacy explained. To my resentment.

"No way."

"It's totally awesome. He's like a celebrity now," Stacy said.

Okay, so my approval of her went up only a tad.

"It's Kurt, and it's no big deal, really." I held out a hand for the girl to shake.

"Tara. Nice to meet you Kurt," she said and I took her soft hand. Maybe she would go out with me was the thought I had right there and then, maybe it's because I'm a sad single guy and she's a girl showing me compulsory attention.

"How about I get you girls some shots and I'll let you party. I've got another book to write." I tried.

A barrage of screams blared through me and I slid off my stool.

"But you've gotta stay and have a shot, I'm getting married," Stacy demanded.

"Just one?" Tara asked and fluttered her very probably false eye lashes at me.

"Tequila?" I asked the honorary girlfriend for what was supposed to be a drink.

This 'drink' then turned into a strangling rendition of Rihanna; 2-for-1 cocktails thanks to Douglas, some Madonna and Bon Jovi, two more tequila shots and another beer. This all finished with a team effort of 'We are the champions'. Somehow, they propped me up centre stage and even though the room seemed to spin and my leg twitched again, I managed an air punch finish which was followed by the main bar lights coming back on.

"I hate to be the bearer of bad news ladies, but it's closing time," Douglas announced. He had already begun to stack stools on tables, as the team harmony of groaning disapproval came his way.

Just as quickly as the storm of high pitched screaming had come, it blew away and was out of the doors. I couldn't even remember getting a goodbye or a thanks. Right then I had my own problems, like navigation and basic functions.

"Looks like you had a good night Kurtis," Douglas smirked nearby, I couldn't really tell where as my head flopped to one side.

"The best nights always come from nowhere," he chuckled.

"Yeah," I agreed with shallow breaths.

"What have I told you about not coming here anymore?" Douglas barked in a change of tone.

"Huh?" I asked through one side of my mouth.

"You know I'm always gonna drop by 'D-man'," purred the friendly voice of a woman I knew.

Laura Owens or nicknamed 'Big L', all her own idea, made her way to the bar. This larger African American lady used to work the door here at the Drunken Poet's Society. My impaired vision caught her eye as she began to help stack the chairs on a table.

"My shift down at the harbour starts in an hour and you're on my route. Probably where the 'Daddy bought me a Mercedes' crew are headed to next," she added.

I caught sight of her looking up and out at Stacy's gang. They'd stumbled up the steep concrete steps. Even steeper the drunker you got, trust me.

"How much did they drink? Oh crap, Kurt is here, so they're gonna be a pain in my fat ass."

"Hey, Big L," I said over another burp. "Your ass isn't fat, it's great. I'm gonna need your help, again." I held out both arms like a kid ready for bed.

"Again? Damn, can't you cut this guy off, D-man?" Laura asked.

"He's me only customer and it started off as a few quiet drinks. But tonight, I've got takings. Now get outta here before I pay you," Douglas said.

"I guess we're doing this again. That's only coz I haven't worked my legs this week yet."

She scooped me up in her big arms. Was this weird? To me it was the norm, here's this bouncer girl who would carry me back home when I drank too much.

"See ya later Douglas," I cheered over Laura's shoulder.

"Damn you're smelling fine girl," I added and rested my head on her.

"Full of compliments tonight, aren't we? Let me guess tequila?" Laura asked.

We moved to the door.

"You know me so well." I grinned back at her. "Where would I be without the Big L? Big L by name and Big L by nature. You're the LBGT saint of a character in my somewhat boring life story." The breeze of outside hit me and I lurched slightly before burping loudly.

"You gonna chuck, you gonna chuck?" Laura demanded as she held me forward like a puking kid.

"I'm good, I'm good, it's just the fresh air," I mumbled and settled back.

We moved up the first steps towards the street.

"These are my best threads son. You don't wanna be puking all over them."

"Security guard is totally your colour Laura, and that's not a race thing that's just fact..."

"Do I need to drop your ass again Kurt?"

"No, no, not this early in our journey. Maybe onto that trash pile if you have to, but please don't," I begged.

Everything spun around as we moved into the main apartment building.

"And keep the noise down, most normal people are sleeping at this time on a Monday, Jesus."

"You have to understand Laura, most of my neighbours, they are assholes. Especially that bitch opposite me. Damn it my leg is twitching again. If I stretch out it goes away." I awkwardly spread myself out as Laura tried to carry me up the apartment block stairs.

"You gonna answer that?"

"Huh?" I asked.

"The vibrating in your damn leg Kurt, it's your cell phone, someone's calling you."

"Oh yeah, so that's what it is." I closed one eye to get a better view at my cell's glowing screen, as I went to answer the call it ended and then I read it.

"Five missed calls? What the actual shit? Shit, shit, shit, shit in a s sandwich, shit on a stick," I swore.

I was moving into that drunken over talking phase, even though I could hardly hold my head up.

"It's Jordy, she's tried to call me twelve thousand times."

"Didn't you guys break up like five months ago. Screw her man," Laura said, and we hit another floor.

"Yeah, that's the one thing I didn't do."

"I know because I carried you that night as well. You mainlined red wine if I recall, then we watched DVDs on wrestling until dawn."

"You see that's why your perfect for me," I grinned, playing up to the joke crush that I had on the probably only reliable safe person I knew.

"My grip suddenly feels loose," she threatened good humouredly.

"We've watched cage matches together! Please don't betray me," I begged.

Without even getting out of breath she carried me up to my floor. Just when I was about to slip out of consciousness, she spoke;

"Looks like you got a visitor Kurt."

"Huh, I'm here?" I asked and my vision angled down to a swathe of red covering the floor.

"Somebody spill something down here?"

"Nah, son, they were put here intentionally. Rose petals and they're leading right into your half-open apartment door," Laura said.

"I really should change my locks or even better, actually try using them."

"Want me to go in first. Secure the area?"

"Nah, Big L, we can handle it. To the apartment!" I shouted and raised a charging finger.

We moved all two steps and Laura pushed the door.

"I've been waiting for you," came a soft voice. My almost stroke-like condition didn't allow me to look straight forward. Okay, maybe stroke is an overstatement, especially if you're a stroke patient, however I had lost most of my functions right about then.

My eyes staggered along the wooden floor of the apartment and up to some bare legs. Who's this I thought? With all hopes forward, maybe Stacy had brought the party upstairs. Continuing to look up, I saw a relatively decent pair of knees and then the snake! The snake tattoo, 'no! Oh god no'.

"Jordy," I cried out in a semi-conscious slur.

"Didn't you guys break up five months ago? Damn." Laura shook her head.

Jordy stood there in just a zip-up sweater; my hooded zip-up sweater!

"I want you back Kurt, so I let myself in," she said so innocently. Don't let that fool you. The snake is the real deal in terms of her personality.

"And I found your turquoise sweater. It's so comfy and I thought you wouldn't mind."

"Oh, he minds. You weren't here for ground zero girl. We watched wrestling until sunrise," Laura added.

"Oh, maybe I made a mistake. I see you're with Lauren now then, I thought you were..."

"It's Laura! And yeah, you thought that right..."

"No, no, no. It's not like that, she's… and I'm… well, we're not together. Okay?" I growled, probably at the wrong person and she let me drop to the hard floor.

"Laura?" I moaned in pain. "Big L, come on girl, I didn't mean it like that," I cried.

"What about the cage matches?" I called, as Laura slammed the door shut behind her.

My winded body tried to turn towards the girl in only my turquoise sweater.

"Come to bed Kurtis, I promise I will make it worth your while," she said, blowing me a cliché kiss.

"I'm… already… there!" I groaned, doing my best to drag my numb body towards the glass bedroom doors. 'Come on Wiseman, pull'.

"Please wait." My hand reached out. God, I was so drunk.

"Have you been drinking again?" she asked in an immediate change of tone.

"Huh? What made you think that?" I rolled over on the floor and crashed into my armchair. Somehow, I managed to prop myself up against it. There I sat, slumped at an angle which would ache for a week, and then I tried to talk.

"Look, Jordy. We had a thing, but that's all it was, just a thing, and that was a 'was', not an 'is'," I slurred. "I knew you were sleeping with that dude the whole time man. Not cool, not cool man."

"I've changed Kurt, he made me realise how lucky I really was." Jordy pleaded.

"Why? Could he drink more than you?" I laughed.

"What is that supposed to mean? I came here tonight, I even tried to call you."

"Well I ain't hard to find," I argued and couldn't keep my eyes open anymore.

"You know what? Fine then. If you don't want me, I was with someone else anyway." Jordy said and that was the last thing I consciously heard her say.

"Uh huh, that's great, just leave me my sweater before you go…" And like that, I was no longer for this world, but rushing head long into a weird dream land which seemed to make my head ache more and more.

Chapter 2: Second Round

I really hate booze and let me tell you; there aren't many things I hate more in this world than what that poison does to you. What's more, let us not overlook the comparable contrast of how the last round opened, that's literature for you. The glinting sunlight bruised my aching existence the next morning and I knew I'd moved into the remorseful phase. I groaned, not in pain of the headache, but from the holy hell of what happened last night. The snake girl burned into my mind.

That witch had even found my prized turquoise sweater and used it to encase her dirty cheating body. I really hoped she hadn't taken it and then my answer came. My pained neck and head brushed over the soft familiar material and momentarily I opened one dry eye. She had probably tried to throw it in my face on the way out and now most of the turquoise fabric had become my pillow.

I plumped the makeshift head rest and rolled over on my flat wooden floor bed. If I lay still, the pain and dizziness might go away.

I winced yet again as I recalled how I'd spoken to Laura last night.

Remorseful embarrassment does that to you, sometimes. Then my mind tried to drift past the drunken events I'd gotten myself in.

"I dunno Lou, he looks shot to pieces." The peaceful silence was broken by a man's Brooklyn accent.

"I doubt he's got any more talk in him."
"All that liquor didn't just make him talk Vinny, he sang. Pissed that big broad off in the process. Let's face it kid, we've got no hope with him like this," muttered another guy, his voice deeper than the first and he seemed older.

"Huh?" I opened the one eye again.

With blurry vision, I saw two shady figures standing over me. One of them with a smoking cigarette, the other taller with a trilby hat on his head.

"He's thinking of doing 'super heroes' next. No chance of a sequel for us anytime soon then," Vinny said. His high-pitched buzzing voice bothering me.

"Guess it will always be One Night for us," Lou said.

"Go away," I groaned and attempted to roll over.

"You're the boss, Boss," the deep voice of Lou added.

"Yeah, we was just remindin' you of last night's conquests, mainly pissing off the Big L."

"I didn't mean to," I groaned, my fingers pressing over the pride badge on the inside of my zip-up.

"You know, guys like you need to be wearing that badge on the outside if you want it to count." I could almost feel Vinny's judging frown.

"Why are you here?" I growled.

"Somebody's gotta act as your alarm clock. And you created us, remember?"

The fellas from New York shuffled over to my big writing desk, the place where they were made. Sweet silence then ruled again as I blocked out the conscience made up of those two debt collectors.

"Alarm clock," I chuckled, it was then a wounding realisation hit me. It was morning!

Every internal muscle lurched me up and forward from the torture rack that was my painful floor bed. The time; 8.15am. I should have got up half an hour ago. Guess I was gonna be late, screw it, I'll think of something on the way.

The bass of shouting reverberated through my walls from the hall, whilst I headed to the bathroom.

"Fine, then go! And don't come back!" The bitch opposite me shouted. It was her usual running gag of breaking up with her equally asshole boyfriend who owned an abusively loud car.

He yelled something back before a loud crash resonated across my floor.

"Domestic abuse? Our subjects are evolving," I noted out loud and twisted the shower dial.

The rush of hot water did nothing to numb the ache, and I laughed at how those bachelorette party girls dragged me up on the stage to sing last night.

"2-for-1 cocktails," I chuckled to myself before moving on to drying. For a second, I caught a glimpse of myself in the half-steamed mirror. Looking back at me was the fine figure I had become. A solid two-pack sat below a sad set of pecks. I poked the bags underneath each eye and convinced myself that there was no time to worry about my ticking body clock. Not that I was trying for kids any time soon.

"Late, late, late... latte?" I asked myself. Maybe I had the time for a vanilla latte on the way to my bus stop.

Clothes on? Check. Phone, wallet and keys? Check. Turquoise hoody up? Check. Dignity? Down in the bar, lost three years ago along with most of my savings. I grabbed my rucksack and headed out the door.

The creak of floorboards opposite me stirred me into action and I flung the door open, feeling immediately exposed. My hands worked at putting the key into my lock; that should keep the Jordy-type snake girls out.

Another feeling of frowning eyes burned through my hood, this time from a real person not one from my conscious. She was standing there, that bitch from opposite.

"Morning," I croaked and kept my head firmly down. Avoid eye contact, I mean who likes their neighbours anyway?

"Hey, looks like somebody picked a fight with a florist out here last night," she snarled.

My eyes caught sight of blonde hair and a pencil skirt. I looked down at the rose petals left by Jordy.

"You know anything about this mess?" The bitch demanded.

"Nope. Well, have a good day," I said and coursed away with her eyes following me.

"My boyfriend slipped on them. My ex-boyfriend, I mean. Asshole. He deserved it."

There came the kind of silence that only follows conversation killing words. I stopped, which made it worse.

"Anyway, see ya soon Kurt."

"Cool." I added and made for the stairs.

Why did I call this girl the bitch across the hall? No reason. In fact I didn't even know her, only that occasionally she would flip out and go full-on marital with the guy she was seeing. From that I thought she was a bitch and considering she lived across the hall, I just merged those concepts. Some things are what they are.

Now why am I mentioning the bitch across the hall? Well friends, she just may happen to be a somewhat relevant character in this little word party that we got going on here. I'll ask the questions here and answer them later during the important plot points, that's called resolve. You can have that lesson for free, or for however much you paid to read these words.

There's no way to make a hungover Tuesday morning bus commute across Bay Valley interesting. So, I won't mention it further. Time stood north of 9.30am by the time I walked into the wide blacked-out glass building that was Liqui-tech. My sneakers squeaked on their shiny marble floors and even in my lateness, I chose not to take the elevator for claustrophobic reasons. I zagged to the staircase door.

I work in Brand Outreach, which probably sounds like some bullshit right? For Liqui-tech, a big-time player in science stuff. I say 'stuff' because I don't know half the crap they make or do. Maybe you're thinking I should probably know something about the company to work in 'Brand Outreach' right? Well I haven't been found out yet and let's keep that our little secret because the pay is steady, and the conditions are relaxed.

So, what is it that I do in this modern work place for seven and half hours a day? Not much, but here's the story kids; next time you find yourself sitting in the reception of some stuffy office, look out for the typical brochure that's sitting on a glass table as you wait for your job interview, or even better, those work place posters scattered around.

Just think of that typical image, the one where there's normally a suited-up guy with a smarmy smile, he may even be holding a clipboard or smiling down at a computer with some false results. Opposite him is the youngish looking broad smiling. Maybe she's leaning over him or the desk. He desperately wants to make more than small talk to her but goes home at night and cries himself to sleep, masturbates some more and crawls through life only wondering every now and then how socially inadequate he is.

She on the other hand would wish at least one guy in the office would stop checking out her ass or tits and treat her for what she can do, not what she looks like. She'll stay at the office until seven to prove that and then change into sneakers for the journey home. On the way, she'll pick up a bottle of wine, after all anything over five bucks is all the same anyway, that's what she thinks, and she'll drink it and then move onto the liquor cabinet with high hopes the booze is enough to drown out her depressing spinster life of assholes hitting on her at work.

Specific, right? You see I'm all about the detail, and that picture I painted for you is what I strive to succeed in all the Liqui-tech brochures. Putting together a picture like that, with such undertones, is half my imagination filling in the gaps and the other half tricking those two 'model' employees that they are the face of the company. I also update the website and social media stuff using my adept powers of blagging. It's a good gig with very little management interference, the only guy I work with is my manager and he's casual to say the least. As long as I coast out of his way, he coasts out of mine. I mean who in their right mind wants to work, right?

Even our office sits out of sight, at the end of a curved hall next to a cleaning supply cupboard. A single door pane looks into the poorly lit windowless hovel I'll call home for the day. This time around it's darker than usual as the lights are off. Phew, guess me being late will go unnoticed. I pull out my key and open the door.

The two fluorescent lights flicker to life as I enter my print room-type place. By the door sits Marcus' desk; empty and deserted. He'll check emails and spend the day reclining, maybe even offer to show me a YouTube video, all this to look forward to when he finally gets in.

Thank the lord he wasn't there to see me shuffle my hungover ass to the desk stuffed behind a shelf unit, although he wouldn't notice or give a shit, that's real management for you.

Some days we don't even talk, maybe a nod or grunt is enough. Take that personnel and your death by PowerPoint seminars about 'communication in the work place'.

"And breathe," I said, knowing that nobody else had noticed my lateness. Maybe I could even catch a couple of winks. My sneakers crossed each other up on the paper strewn desk and I leant back. Just when everything had settled, the door burst open.

Marcus Preston had made it in, late like me. His jolly frame breezed towards me and my horizontal state.

"I was late as well," I said.

I watched the guy kind of moonwalk with his shoes squeaking on the plastic floor.

"What have we got today then?" he asked and I shrugged.

"Good, that's how I like it. Hang tight kid, we may get some work this month, but I'm not holding out."

Truth is, Marcus is a good dude. He's what you call a 'lifer' in the company and has worked every position going. So, he knows his stuff. He shuffled away and back to his desk. His seat clunked as he reached full recline.

My office chair sprung forward as I reached up to grab my headphones; maybe the pounding of music will pound out the actual pounding in my head.

"Actually…"

Shit. I guess there's something he wants me to do. Again, came the squeak of moonwalking shoes and Marcus busted a move my way.

"We got an email last night. A new demo is happening downstairs. The big boss has requested social media coverage and we all know that the jokers in our marketing department can't read, write or spell." He handed me a ruffled piece of paper which had clearly been screwed up and trashed. There was even the resemblance of a penis shape drawn in thick pen…

Enjoy the rest of the Teleporter here:

https://www.amazon.com/dp/B07CKFXDP4

Open Evening
Lee Hall

Sometimes you don't get to choose where you are placed in the collective ecosystem of a high school.

Luke Hartford spends his days on the fringes of social inadequacy. A normal day at his small down American High School can be described as horrific. That is until events take a turn for the worse. After a vision, Luke realises there is something other than the horror of trying to fit in lurking just under the surface.

A mysterious stranger arrives in town and the teachers are acting weirder than normal. Soon enough Luke and an unlikely team of allies must fight their way towards survival, even if they don't really know who to trust. The question is, who will survive the Open Evening?

"If I can see you, they can see you."

'The best read of the year...'

'I was hooked...'

'Entertaining, engaging; a real page turner.'

Available now to download and in paperback.

https://www.amazon.co.uk/dp/B01M07N4SA

Darke Blood
Lee Hall

"There are more than shadows lurking in the darkness of those trees."

Blake Malone is in search of a new start and arrives in the remote forest town of Darke Heath. The memory of his past mysteriously becomes a blur as he discovers this place isn't what it seems.

Malone shares a romantic encounter with a woman named Caitlyn and she reveals herself to be a 'creature of the night'. He learns of her story which intertwines with the history of the 'Heath'. Together they must face the evil forces of vampirism and witchcraft that await them in the Darke forest.

But just who is Blake Malone? That's something even he must fight to discover. Because 'you've never known true darkness...'

'Excellent story...'

'If you were to only read one new vampire book I would recommend Darke Blood...'

'Not your average vampire novel!'

Available now to download and in paperback.
https://www.amazon.com/dp/B072LPNX3P

Cemetery House
Lee Hall

The survivors from Open Evening are back for their next chapter and together they must face life after high school. Led by a man named Twister, they learn of his origins and where he came from; a place that suffered a similar fate to their hometown. Accompanied by his newly formed crew, Twister must return home to face the demons of his past, only now the town has been converted into a horror-themed amusement park. With a 'purge' imminent in the park, those who survived high school must look for answers as they take on their next challenge. The world of work can be filled with horror hiding just beneath the surface which has returned yet again for the roller coaster ride that is Cemetery House. So get ready to run, think, fight and live, because 'survival was just the beginning…'

'Page turner…'

Available now to download and in paperback.
https://www.amazon.co.uk/Cemetery-House-Lee-Hall-ebook/dp/B07JZ6KTBL

Printed in Great Britain
by Amazon